Philomena
The Cat Who
Thinks She's
a Dog

Philomena
The Cat Who Thinks She's a Dog

Jessie Wall

Illustrated by Emily Stanbury

WACKY BEE

Published in 2016 by Wacky Bee Books

Wacky Bee Books
Shakespeare House, 168 Lavender Hill, London SW11 5TG

www.wackybeebooks.com

ISBN 978-0-9931109-2-4 (paperback)
ISBN 978-0-9931109-7-9 (ebook)

British Library Cataloguing in Publication Data
A CIP catalogue record for this book is available from
the British Library

Set in Goudy by Head & Heart Publishing Services
Printed by Dinefwr Press, Wales

To Roberta - C. B.

To Ian, Jenny, Harry
& Kate - E. S.

With special thanks to
Cherith Baldry

Contents

1

Philomena Finds a New Home

Philomena's whiskers twitched. Her stomach felt as if it was full of mice, chasing each other's tails.

I'm going to a new home today, she thought.

She felt a bit sad to be leaving her mother Moby, her sisters and her brother Geronimo, but mostly she was excited.

I hope my new family are nice, she thought.

When Philomena heard the doorbell ring, she thought of going to hide under the kitchen cupboard. But instead she sat up straight. She was glad that Moby had given her a specially thorough lick to make sure she looked extra smart.

Mrs Plunkett and Dylan
came into the kitchen with
three other people following
them.

"Philomena, this is Mr
and Mrs Simpkins and their
daughter Sophie," said Mrs

Plunkett. "You're going to go
and live with them."

Dylan scooped up
Philomena and gave her a
goodbye stroke.

"Take care," he said.
"Mind you behave yourself."

"I'm sure she will," said Mrs Simpkins. "Do you like her, Sophie? She's such a cute little cat."

Philomena pricked up her ears. A cute little **WHAT**?

Sophie took Philomena from Dylan and cuddled her close.

"I love her already," she said. "She's the best little cat in the world."

Yes, I did hear it right, thought Philomena as she rode with Sophie to the Simpkins' car.

All the Plunkett family, Moby and the other kittens and Geronimo came to the door to see her off. Geronimo waved his tail like a big, hairy rope.

"Wave goodbye, little cat," said Sophie.

These people seem nice enough, thought Philomena, *but they must be a bit stupid. Geronimo's my brother, and he's a dog, so why can't they get it that I'm no cat? I'm a* **DOG!**

2

Philomena Goes Shopping

Sophie took Philomena
into the sitting room and
showed her a basket with a
soft cushion inside. Next to
the basket was a bowl full of
delicious mousy chunks.

This is great, thought
Philomena as she crouched
down and tucked in. *I'm going
to enjoy living here.*

Then Sophie fastened a collar around Philomena's neck. It had pink, glittery bows on it and a silver disc dangling from the front. Philomena thought it felt weird, and scraped at it with one paw.

"No, Philomena," said Sophie. "You have to wear it in case you get lost."

Then Philomena
remembered how Dylan
had put a collar and lead on
Geronimo to take him for a
walk.

Oookaaay, she thought.
*Maybe they realise that I'm a
dog after all.*

But Sophie didn't bring
a lead. Instead she plopped
Philomena into her dolls'
sleeping basket and then
wheeled them both along to
the shops with Mrs Simpkins.

I'll never live this down,
thought Philomena.

The old man selling
newspapers at the corner
bent down to stroke
Philomena.

"That's a pretty
little cat you've
got there," he
said.

"What a lovely cat!" said
the lady in the bakery.

"Have you tried this new cat food?" the supermarket assistant asked Mrs Simpkins. "My cat loves it."

When Philomena got home she leaped out of the doll's basket and tore off the collar with the pink glittery bows.

What's wrong with people? she wondered as she raced across the garden. *Can't they see that I'm a dog? It's as clear as strawberry ice cream!*

She dived under a holly
bush to think.

*I'm not putting up with
this,* she decided. Her eyes
narrowed and her whiskers
bristled. *I've got to prove to
everyone that I'm a dog...but how?*

3

Philomena Meets the Neighbours

Next day Sophie picked up
Philomena and took her
into the garden of the house
next door. A tall boy came
running to meet them.

He wore ripped jeans and
a T-shirt with a picture of a
skull on it. His baseball cap
was back to front. He had
studs in his ears and a ring
through his nose.

"Hi, Jazz," said Sophie. "This is my new kitten Philomena."

He looks a bit scary, thought Philomena, but before she could run away Jazz was tickling her under her chin.

"She's so cool," he said with a big grin. "I guess it's time she met Bandit."

It was then that Philomena noticed a dog digging in one of the flowerbeds, sending up a spray of earth. When Jazz whistled, the dog looked up and came trotting towards them carrying a bone in his jaws.

He had a chunky body and a broad head. His jaws opened wide as he dropped the bone. Philomena could see his lolling tongue and a whole mouthful of teeth.

He looks even scarier than Jazz, she thought.

"Now say hi to Bandit," said Sophie, putting Philomena down in front of the dog.

Bandit bent his head and gave Philomena a sniff.

Philomena slid her claws out.

Don't you dare try anything, you big mutt, she thought.

Then Bandit stretched out his tongue and gave her a sloppy lick around her ears.

Yuck! she thought to herself, backing off and shaking her head.

"He's only playing," said Sophie, laughing. "There's nothing to be scared of. Bandit is a friendly dog."

"He's a bit too friendly," said Jazz. "Mum and Dad bought him to be a guard dog, but he doesn't even bark when people come to the door. Dad says he's not a proper dog."

Sophie reached out to Bandit and rumpled his ears.

"Of course he's a proper dog," she said. "He can fetch a ball, and beg for treats, and he was just burying a bone in your garden. That's what dogs do."

"Yeah," said Jazz, "he's a great dog. But if he can't act a bit fiercer, I don't think Mum and Dad will want to keep him. Honestly, I think Dad would be happier if he bit the postman!"

Philomena pricked up her ears.

So **THAT'S** *what I have to do to prove that I'm a dog. Chase balls, eat dog treats and show an interest in bones. Easy!*

4

How Did It All Go Wrong?

Jazz kicked a ball across the garden.

"Fetch, Bandit!" he called.

But Bandit just sat down and refused to move.

Here's my chance, thought Philomena.

Philomena raced after the ball, but the ball was too big for her to pick it up in her mouth. Instead, she patted it with her paws, dribbling it across the lawn to Sophie's feet.

Bandit watched her with a puzzled face.

Haven't you ever seen a dog fetch a ball before? thought Philomena.

"Hey, that's awesome!" Jazz laughed. "She should play for United."

Sophie bent over and picked up the ball.

"Clever girl!" she said. "Anybody would think you were a dog."

*Well that's because I **am** a dog,* thought Philomena. *Hurray, my plan is working!*

In the next few days
Philomena stuck to her plan.
She played the ball game
again with Sophie. She sat up
and begged for a biscuit.

Everyone thought she was really cute. But they still didn't understand that she was a dog.

I have to try harder, thought Philomena. *I have to do more doggy things. But what other things do dogs do?*

Luckily Bandit was on hand to help her. He was far too lazy to behave like a dog himself but he knew exactly what dogs were **meant** to do.

He taught Philomena how
to chase the postman...

He taught her how to
growl at Jazz...

And he taught her how to
bury bones in the garden.

But somehow Mr and Mrs
Simpkins didn't think she
was cute any more.

"I've never known such a
naughty little cat," said Mr
Simpkins. "If she goes on
like this we definitely can't
keep her."

5

Trouble in the Night

Philomena lay curled up in her basket in the kitchen. Her cushion was soft and comfortable, but she couldn't sleep. She had never felt so miserable in her life.

*They **still** think I'm a cat,* she thought despairingly. *And now they don't want me any more.*

Then Philomena heard a noise coming from the sitting room next to the kitchen. She sat up and listened. When the noise came again she got out of her basket, padded into the hall, and poked her head around the sitting-room door.

Philomena's eyes widened and her jaw dropped open in amazement. A strange man was in the sitting room, pulling out the plugs from the Simpkins' television.

A *burglar!*

For a moment Philomena was frozen in shock. Then she realised this was her big chance.

I have to guard the house, she thought. *I have to show everybody that I'm a guard dog, and if I help them catch the burglar, they'll want to keep me.*

She raced up the stairs and started scratching at Mr and Mrs Simpkins' bedroom door. She let out her loudest yowls. But there was no sound from inside the room.

Wake up! she thought. *You're being burgled!*

When there was still
no reply Philomena tried
yowling at Sophie's door.
Sophie's sleepy voice drifted
back to her.

"Go to bed, Philomena.
This isn't the time to play."

Rats! Philomena said to
herself. *Now what do I do?*

6

A Friend in Need

Philomena raced back down the stairs and looked into the sitting room again. The patio doors were open and the burglar was staggering down the path, carrying the Simpkins' television. A white van was parked in the road outside the gate.

Oh, no! He's getting away!

Philomena dashed outside and scrambled over the fence into Jazz's garden. When she jumped down onto the lawn she stopped and sniffed. Then she followed Bandit's scent around the side of the house where she found him snoring in his kennel.

Philomena prodded him with one paw.

Wake up!

Bandit let out a grunt and opened his eyes. He blinked at her for a moment, then closed his eyes again.

Philomena prodded him harder. Bandit didn't even twitch an ear.

*You **will** wake up!* thought Philomena. *We have a burglar to catch.*

This time she jumped on top of Bandit and tickled him with her claws. He jerked awake, lurched to his paws, and let out a long howl.

Bandit gave her an injured look, as if he was asking, *What did you do that for? I thought we were friends.*

Bouncing up and down in front of him, Philomena gave him a last swipe on his nose. Then she raced off down the garden path towards the gate. Bandit galloped after her, barking all the way.

Upstairs in the house, Jazz's dad threw open a window. "Bandit, stop that racket!" he

yelled.

"No, Dad!" That was Jazz's voice.

"Something's wrong."

Windows were opening in the Simpkins' house, too. Then the door flew wide open and Mrs Simpkins dashed outside with her mobile phone in her hand.

"Get me the police!" she shouted.

But when Philomena reached the gate she saw that the burglar had finished loading the television into his van. He was closing the doors.

He's going to get away!

7

Philomena's Secret

As the burglar hurried to the front of his van, Philomena hurled herself after him. She dived between his ankles. The burglar tripped over her and came crashing to the ground.

He almost landed on
Philomena, but she darted
away just in time and hid
underneath the van.

Phew! she thought. *He
nearly squashed me flat.*

Mrs Simpkins and Jazz's
dad grabbed the burglar and
sat on him until a police car
came tearing up the
road with
its siren
wailing
and its
blue light
flashing.

Peering out from underneath the van, Philomena saw Jazz run up with Bandit, who had stopped barking. The dog looked confused, as if he still didn't know what was happening.

"Bandit gave the alarm," Jazz said to his dad. "You can't say that he isn't a proper guard dog now."

Jazz's dad nodded. "You're right, son," he said.

"So we're keeping him?" said Jazz.

"Of course we are!" Philomena sighed.

Bandit would still be asleep if it wasn't for me, she thought. I mean, I'm glad he can stay and all, but it's me who's the real guard dog, not him.

Then she saw Sophie, peering at her under the van and holding out her hand.

"You can come out now, Philomena," she said.

Philomena crawled out from her hiding place and jumped onto Sophie's lap. Mrs Simpkins came over and stroked her.

"She caught the burglar," said Sophie. "He would have escaped if she hadn't tripped him up."

"She's a clever, brave little cat," Mrs Simpkins agreed. "She can stay with us for ever."

Well, that's good, thought Philomena. *But I guarded the house and caught a burglar, and they're still calling me a cat.*

Then she snuggled in to Sophie's woolly dressing gown. A deep purr welled up from inside her chest.

It's pretty nice being a cat, she decided. *I guess I could pretend if it makes Sophie happy. I know that I'm really a dog, but I think it'll have to be my secret!*

THE END

Geronimo
The Dog Who Thinks He's a Cat

If you liked reading about Philomena you'll love reading about Geronimo as well.

Geronimo's mum has so many puppies she doesn't know what to do. So when Geronimo decides to leave home for a better life, he enters a great, big, scary world where he doesn't know who he is...and has no idea what his is either!

What they said about *Geronimo*:
"See what happens in this hilarious, touching story with expressive illustrations and a lovely twist at the end. Short novel with large print and illustrations on every page making it a bridge from picture book to novel." *Primary Times*

WACKÝ BEE

Wacky Bee is a very small company but that doesn't mean that our ideas are small. Far from it! We have big ideas for our books. And because we're small and independent, it means that we can put those big ideas into action in exactly the way that we want...and have a lot of fun while we're at it.

Find out more about
Wacky Bee at
www.wackybeebooks.com